Contents

Joey   Tom

Bird Crazy

Felice Arena and Phil Kettle

illustrated by
Susy Boyer

RISING STARS

First Published in Great Britain by
RISING STARS UK LTD 2006
22 Grafton Street, London, W1S 4EX

For more information visit our website at:
www.risingstars-uk.com

British Library Cataloguing in Publication Data

A CIP record for this book is available from the British Library.

ISBN: 978-1-84680-056-6

First published in 2006 by
MACMILLAN EDUCATION AUSTRALIA PTY LTD
627 Chapel Street, South Yarra 3141

Visit our website at www.macmillan.com.au or
go directly to www.macmillanlibrary.com.au

Associated companies and representatives throughout the world.

Series created by Felice Arena and Phil Kettle
Project management by Limelight Press Pty Ltd
Cover and text design by Lore Foye
Illustrations by Susy Boyer

Printed in China

UK Editorial by Westcote Computing Editorial Services

CHAPTER 1

Birds of Prey

Best friends Tom and Joey are
spending the weekend at Tom's
uncle's farm. After a busy morning
of milking cows, the boys watch a
wildlife show about birds on TV.

Joey "Wow! Did you see that?"

Tom "Yes. That was so amazing! That falcon just swooped down and picked up the rabbit."

Joey "Poor little rabbit."

Tom "Mmmm! Takeaway rabbit for the whole family—that's what the falcon's thinking."

Joey "That's disgusting!"

Tom "Too bad they couldn't get any chips with that."

Joey "You're gross!"

Joey and Tom watch some more.

Tom "I thought this bird show was going to be boring. But it isn't! These birds of prey are amazing."

Joey "Birds of prey?"

Tom "Yes. What do you think we've
been watching? You do know what
birds of prey are, don't you?"

Joey "Yes. Who doesn't know that?"

Tom "Then what are they?"

Joey "Er ..."

Tom "See, you don't know."

Joey "Yes, I do they're, er, birds that like to swoop and poop on nuns."

Tom bursts out laughing.

Tom "Good one! But they also hunt for small animals. They're killer birds. They love to eat guts and gizzards and ..."

Joey "OK! OK! I understand! They eat more than seeds!"

Tom "Hey, do you know what I'm thinking?"

Joey "What?"

Tom "Guess."

Joey "You're starving?"

Tom "No!"

Joey "*I'm* starving?"

Tom "No! About birds."

Joey "They have feathers?"

Tom "Arrgh! No! I'm thinking let's go and look for our own killer birds."

Joey "Oh! Yes! Cool!"

CHAPTER 2

There's One!

Tom borrows a pen, a writing pad, a camera and a pair of binoculars from his uncle. Joey follows a few steps behind.

Joey "What's all that for?"

Tom "So we can keep records of all the birds we spot—just like the man on the TV show."

Joey "This is going to be great."

The boys go outside and begin their search. Tom gives Joey the pen and writing pad.

Joey "Do you think we'll see any pelicans?"

Tom "Pelicans? No, we're only looking for birds of prey."

Joey "Pelicans hunt for fish."

Tom "Yes, but they're not evil hunters like eagles or owls."

Joey "Shame. I like pelicans."

The boys walk down a muddy path towards the back of the farm.

Joey "There's one!"

Tom swings around ready to take a photo with the camera.

Tom "That's not a bird of prey. It's only a sparrow."

Joey "So? Sparrows hunt for worms and butterflies and stuff."

Tom "Yes, but they're not the birds we're looking for. But I suppose you had better write it down."

Joey "Look, there's one!"

Tom "Where?"

Joey "It flew into that tree in the middle of the field."

Tom "What was it?"

Joey "I don't know, but it was huge."

Tom "It could be a falcon."

Joey "Really?"

Tom "Yes, I've seen falcons around here before. Let's go."

Joey "Go?"

Tom "We have to get close if we want to take a photo of it. Come on, hurry, before it flies away!"

CHAPTER 3

Shhh! Quiet!

Tom runs out into the empty field towards the tree. Joey chases him.

Joey "Wait! Why are we running? We don't want to scare it off."

Tom suddenly stops. Joey catches up, panting heavily.

Tom "You're right! We don't want to scare it. We should sneak up on it."

Joey "That's what I was thinking."

The boys slowly creep towards the tree.

Joey "Do you think it has a nest up there?"

Tom "It might. Falcons are really clever. Some people keep falcons as pets. They use them for hunting."

Joey "Really? How do you know that?"

Tom "I saw it in a book once. There was this farmer who taught his falcon to do these amazing tricks. He taught it to fetch his hat from a post that was a hundred metres away."

Joey "Cool! Imagine if we had our own falcon."

Tom "Yes, that would be great. I'd get it to defend me from bad people and robbers. I'd shout at them, 'Stop! I wouldn't come closer if I were you!' Then I'd whistle a secret signal. And before you'd know it, 'Claw', that's what I'd call him, would swoop down and scare the bad guys away."

Joey "Cool. I'd use our falcon for tennis."

Tom "Tennis?"

Joey "Yes, who needs ball boys when you've got a falcon! I'd teach my falcon to get all the balls I missed. Then I'd probably become really famous, because every tennis club in the world would want their very own ball-falcons. So, they'd have to call me to train them."

Tom "Now you're dreaming.

Joey Just think how exciting a game of tennis would be!"

Tom Shhh! Did you hear that?"

The boys are only a few steps away from the base of the tree. They look up to see the shadow of a bird rustling in the top branches.

CHAPTER 4

A Great Idea

The boys stand underneath the tree staring into the branches.

Tom "I don't believe it."

Joey "What is it? Is it a falcon?"

Tom "No. It's only a crow!"

Joey "That's a bird of prey, isn't it?"

Tom "No ... er, yes, I think it is. Here, quick, let's swap. You take a photo. Let me write it down in the book."

Tom scribbles down, "Crow spotted in tree. 11.35 a.m. Sat 12 May" on his writing pad. Joey begins to make kissing-like noises. The crow flies away.

Tom "What are you doing?"

Joey "I'm trying to sound like a rabbit."

Tom "Why?"

Joey "Because, that's what falcons like to hunt."

Tom "Oh, yes. That's right."

Joey "Remember on that TV show, it said that falcons have really good hearing. So, if I sound like a rabbit, a falcon might hear me and come looking for it."

Tom "That's it!"

Joey "What's it?"

Tom "Don't move. I've got a great idea."

Tom runs off. He returns with a toy
rabbit, some gardening gloves and a
cardboard box.

Joey "What are you doing?"
Tom "We're going to catch a falcon."
Joey "We are?"

CHAPTER 5

Come and Get It!

Tom walks out into the middle of
the field, away from the tree. While
holding the soft toy rabbit, he slips
on the gardening gloves and then lies
on the ground.

Joey "I still don't understand. What are you doing? How is this going to help us catch a falcon?"

Tom "I told you. This toy rabbit will be a decoy. You cover me in grass, so the falcon won't see me. I'll move the rabbit around and make rabbit noises, like you did before. The falcon will hear me, then it will fly over and will see the toy rabbit. Understand?"

Joey "Sort of. And then what will happen?"

Tom "Well, the falcon will swoop down on the toy rabbit and when it grabs the rabbit with its claws, I'll grab the falcon."

Joey "Ah, and that's why you're wearing gardening gloves?"

Tom "Yes! Because falcon claws are very sharp—sharper than any knives. Falcon claws can slice right through your stomach if they want to."

Joey "Cool. So what am I going to do?"

Tom "You'll be hiding behind the tree with the cardboard box and when I grab the falcon, you'll run out and I'll quickly shove it in the box."

Joey "Then what?"

Tom "Then we have our very own falcon and will be able to teach it tricks, that's what! Now, cover me in grass."

Joey covers Tom in grass and runs off to hide behind the tree. Tom makes rabbit noises for a while but eventually gets bored and falls asleep. Thirty minutes pass before he wakes up.

Tom "Hey, Joey, are you there? I
don't think this is working ... Joey?"

Tom stands and brushes the
grass off himself. He wanders to the
tree to discover that Joey has gone.
Tom makes his way back to the
farmhouse. He is surprised to see
Joey eating at the kitchen table.

Tom "Why did you leave?"

Joey "I got bored waiting. And I didn't want to wake you up. And ..."

Tom "And what?"

Joey "I realised there's only one bird I really love—more than pelicans, sparrows, crows, even more than falcons."

Tom "And what's that?"

Joey picks up a drumstick from his plate and takes a big bite.

Joey "Roast chicken! MMMMMM!!!!!"

binoculars Special magnifying glasses you look through to help you zoom in on something you're watching—like birds flying high in the sky.

claws Not Santa (Claus) but claws! Very sharp, curved nails on a bird's foot.

flock Lots of birds hanging out together are called a flock of birds.

poop Rhymes with swoop, but a lot messier! Birds can poop and fly at the same time.

swoop When a bird sweeps down suddenly through the air (not cleaning with a broom).

Bird-watching Must-dos

☞ Look through as many bird books as you can. You want to be able to tell the difference between a falcon and a crow or a seagull, and a pelican or Donald Duck and Tweety Pie.

☞ Have a pen and a notebook with you at all times you so can record the type of birds you see.

☞ Try to wear colours like green and brown that blend in with bushes and trees. You'll be like a secret commando, and if the birds can't see you, you'll have a better chance of getting a closer look.

☞ Take plenty of food and water with you—bird-watching can last for hours.

☞ Learn how to whisper really well. Bird-watchers whisper a lot so they won't scare the birds away.

☞ If you have a camera and some binoculars, take them with you on your bird-watching adventure. All professional bird-watchers use binoculars.

☞ Never get too close to a nest or disturb it. Mother birds will do anything to protect their eggs or chicks—even if that means attacking you.

☞ Learn how to make some bird calls. Some birds will appear when they hear hoots, whistles, squawks or chirps that sound like their own.

Bird-watching Instant Info

The albatross has one of the largest wingspans of any bird. Its wings can sometimes measure up to 3 metres from one wing tip to the other.

The largest bird on the planet is the ostrich. A male ostrich can grow up to 2.5 metres tall. The ostrich is also the fastest bird on land. It can run as fast as 45 miles per hour.

The largest bird's nest ever recorded was built by a pair of bald eagles, near St. Petersburg, Florida, USA. It was 2.9 metres wide and 6 metres deep.

There are many famous birds on television. These include Big Bird, Tweety Pie, Road Runner and Foghorn Leghorn.

Parrots are great mimics. They can copy the way you talk. Be careful what you say in front of them!

In the United States of America, people celebrate a holiday called Thanksgiving, usually by cooking a large turkey.

Duck feathers and goose feathers are often used as the stuffing for pillows and duvets.

BOYS RULE!
Think Tank

1   What types of bird are Tom and Joey trying to find?

2   What did the boys find in the tree?

3   What says, "Beep, beep" and goes really fast?

4   What would a falcon say if it met a rabbit?

5   What bird looks like it's wearing a tuxedo?

6   A falcon is also a type of car. True or false?

7   What equipment do you need to go bird-watching?

8   Why does Tom make kissing noises?

Answers

8 Tom makes kissing noises so a falcon will think he's a rabbit.

7 You need binoculars and a pen and paper to go bird-watching. Perhaps you're lucky enough to own a camera, too.

6 True. But seeing a falcon driving a falcon ... well, that would be false, but totally cool!

5 A penguin looks like it's wearing a tuxedo.

4 Nice to eat you! (If you said something similar to this then you're also correct.)

3 The TV cartoon character Road Runner, or any type of car.

2 Joey and Tom found a crow in the tree.

1 Tom and Joey are trying to find birds of prey.

How did you score?

- If you got all 8 answers correct, then what are you waiting for? Grab your binoculars! You were made for bird-watching!

- If you got 6 answers correct, then you like birds but only from a distance.

- If you got fewer than 4 answers correct, bird-watching is probably not for you. The closest you'd get to a bird is at Kentucky Fried Chicken.

Felice →   ← Phil

Hi Guys!

We have heaps of fun reading and want you to, too. We both believe that being a good reader is really important and so cool.

Try out our suggestions to help you have fun as you read.

At school, why don't you use "Bird Crazy" as a play and you and your friends can be the actors. Set the scene for your play. Ask your parents if you can bring a camera or a pair of binoculars to school to use as props! There should be plenty of notebooks and pens at school you can use.

So ... have you decided who is going to be Tom and who is going to be Joey? Now, with your friends, read and act out our story in front of the class.

We have a lot of fun when we go to schools and read our stories. After we finish the children all clap really loudly. When you've finished your play your classmates will do the same. Just remember to look out the window—there might be a talent scout from a television channel watching you!

Reading at home is really important and a lot of fun as well.

Take our books home and get someone in your family to read them with you. Maybe they can take on a part in the story.

Remember, reading is fun.

So, as the frog in the local pond would say, Read-it!

And remember, Boys Rule!

When We Were Kids

Felice

Phil

Phil "Did you ever own a bird when you were a kid?"

Felice "No, but I was once attacked by a million seagulls."

Phil "Really? That's terrible."

Felice "You're telling me! It was a nightmare!"

Phil "Why did they attack you? Did you annoy them or something?"

Felice "No. I was wearing a costume promoting a restaurant by the beach."

Phil "That doesn't make sense. Why would a million seagulls attack you then?"

Felice "Because I was dressed as a giant chip!"

42

BOYS RULE!

What a Laugh!

Q What do you get
if you cross a duck
with a firework?

A A firequacker!

BOYS RULE!

Gone Fishing

The Tree House

Golf Legends

Camping Out

Bike Daredevils

Water Rats

Skateboard
Dudes

Tennis Ace

Basketball
Buddies

Secret Agent
Heroes

Wet World

Rock Star

Pirate Attack

Olympic
Champions

Race Car
Dreamers

Hit the Beach

Rotten
School Day

Halloween
Gotcha!

Battle of the
Games

On the Farm